Sleep Tight, Sleepy Bears

First published by Parragon in 2012

Parragon
Queen Street House
4 Queen Street
Bath BA1 1HE, UK
www.parragon.com

Copyright © Parragon Books Ltd 2012
Text © Hollins University

ISBN 978-1-4454-9316-9

Printed in China

Sleep Tight, Sleepy Bears

PaRragon

Bath • New York • Singapore • Hong Kong • Cologne • Delhi
Melbourne • Amsterdam • Johannesburg • Shenzhen

There was a **big** sleepy bear,

and a little sleepy bear.

The big sleepy bear yawned

a great big yawn,

and the little sleepy
bear yawned
a little sleepy yawn.

Then the great
big bear

gave a great big

s t r e t c h ,

and the little sleepy bear gave a little sleepy

s t r e t c h .

Two to watch me through the night.

And two to wake me come daylight.

Softer
and
softer
and
softer.

Then the **big** sleepy bear closed his eyes,

and the little sleepy bear closed his eyes.

And the little sleepy bear
thought of the darkness,
and the starlight,

and the **big** round moon,

and how he'd be sleeping soon.

Then the **big** sleepy bear whispered, "Sleep tight."

And the little sleepy
bear didn't say
a word because he
was sound asleep.